Contents

Chapter 1

On the Job 4

Chapter 2

Helping Oceans 10

Chapter 3

Exploring Oceans 16

More Information 22

CHAPTER 1

On the Job

A huge ship floats in the Antarctic Ocean. It breaks through the sea ice. People lower a yellow robot into the water. It's going to do some **exploring**.

explore: to look at and study something

UNDERWATER ROBOTS

LUKE COLINS

BLACK RABBIT BOOKS

Bolt Jr. is published by Black Rabbit Books
P.O. Box 3263, Mankato, Minnesota, 56002.
www.blackrabbitbooks.com

Grant Gould, designer; Omay Ayres, photo researcher

Title: Underwater robots / by Luke Colins.
Description: Mankato, Minnesota : Black Rabbit Books, [2020] | Series: Bolt Jr. world of robots | Includes bibliographical references and index. | Audience: Age 6-8. | Audience: Grades K to 3. |
Identifiers: LCCN 2019003853 (print) | LCCN 2019004568 (ebook) | ISBN 9781623101732 (e-book) |
ISBN 9781623101671 (library binding) |
ISBN 9781644661116 (paperback)
Subjects: LCSH: Submersibles—Juvenile literature. |
Robots—Juvenile literature.
Classification: LCC VM365 (ebook) | LCC VM365 .C58 2020 (print) | DDC 623.82/74—dc23
LC record available at https://lccn.loc.gov/2019003853

Printed in the United States. 5/19

Image Credits

actu.epfl.ch: EPFL, 10; deepocean.com: Deep Ocean Engineering, 6–7; hawaiipublicradio.org: ELISHA WOOD-CHARLSON / UHM / Hawaii Public Radio, 12; kongsberg.com: Seaglider/Kongsberg, 8–9; manoa.hawaii.edu: WHOI/UH, 18; mbari.org: MBARI, 20–21; news.stanford.edu: DRASSM, 22–23; niu.edu: NIU/Antarctic-Bound Submarine, 5; ranmarine.io: Ran Marine, 13; Shutterstock: Andrey Suslov, Cover, 1; Iakov Filimonov, 4, 21; Martin Nezval, 3, 24; martin_hristov, 16–17 (wreck); Rostislav Ageev, 7; S.Bachstroem, 17 (bot); Zern Liew, 14 (bkgd); washington.edu: Jason Gobat, 11

MUA
HERE TO STAY

DEPTH COMPARISON

35,813 feet (10,916 meters)
how deep one underwater bot can go

Watery Jobs

Bots do many underwater jobs. Some study water. Others clean oceans. Some bots help find hidden animals.

350 feet (107 m)

how deep trained scuba divers can go

PARTS OF A

Seaglider Bot

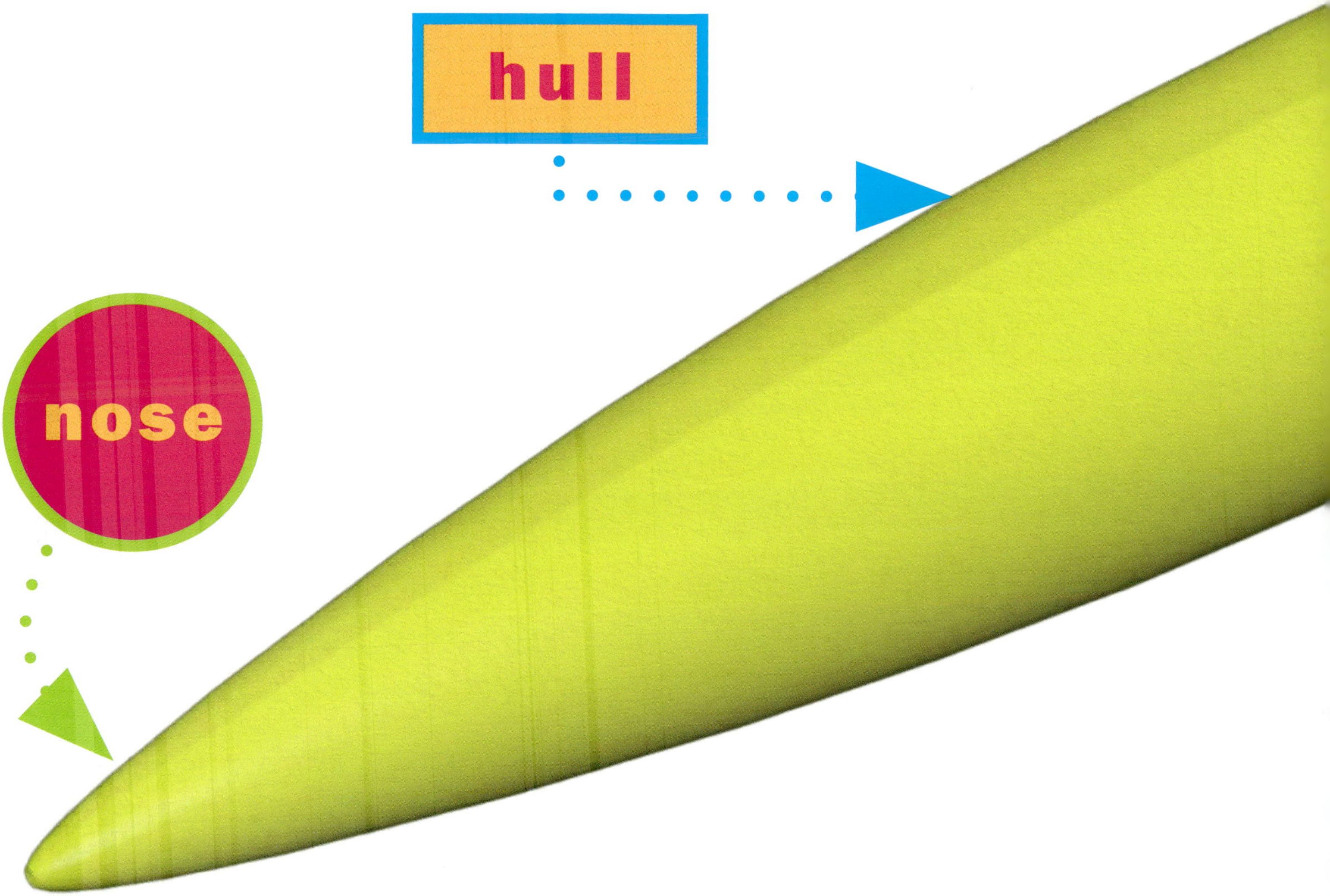

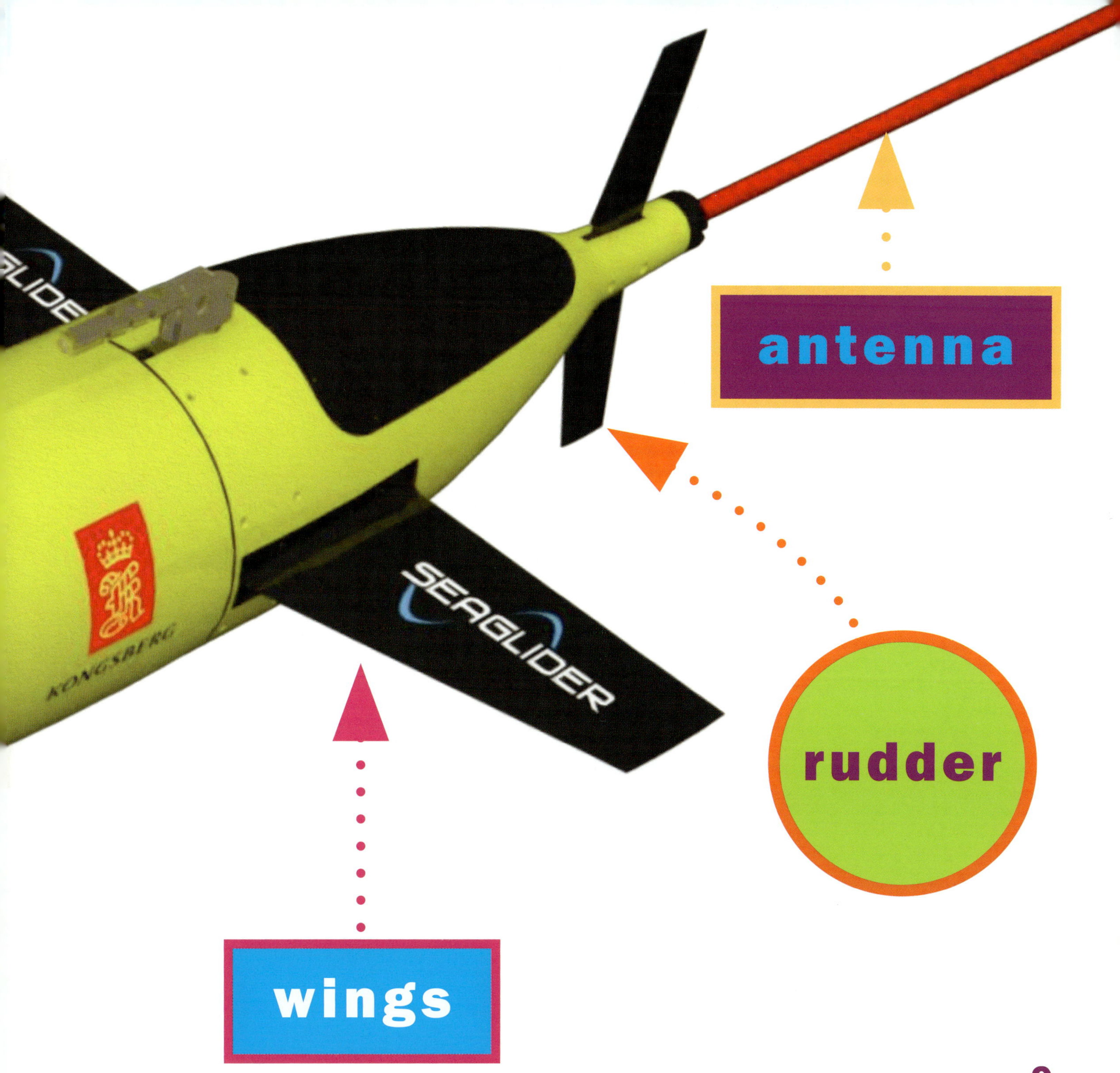
antenna
rudder
wings
SEAGLIDER
KONGSBERG

CHAPTER 2

Helping Oceans

Scientists use bots to learn. Seaglider bots float under sea ice. They **measure** melting ice. Scientists use the information to study **global warming**.

measure: to find out the size or amount of something

global warming: a warming of Earth's air and oceans

FACT

Seaglider's batteries last a year.

Many Uses

A lot of **trash** floats in oceans. Bots are helping clean that up.

Other bots make maps of the sea floor. They take pictures. Some even bring back rocks for testing.

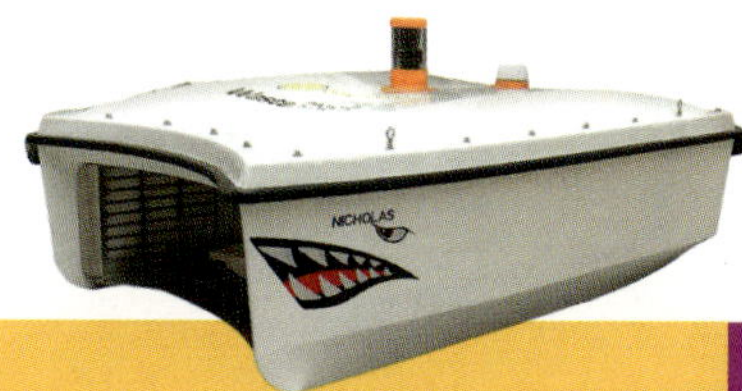

trash: things that are no longer wanted

Underwater Bots In All the Oceans

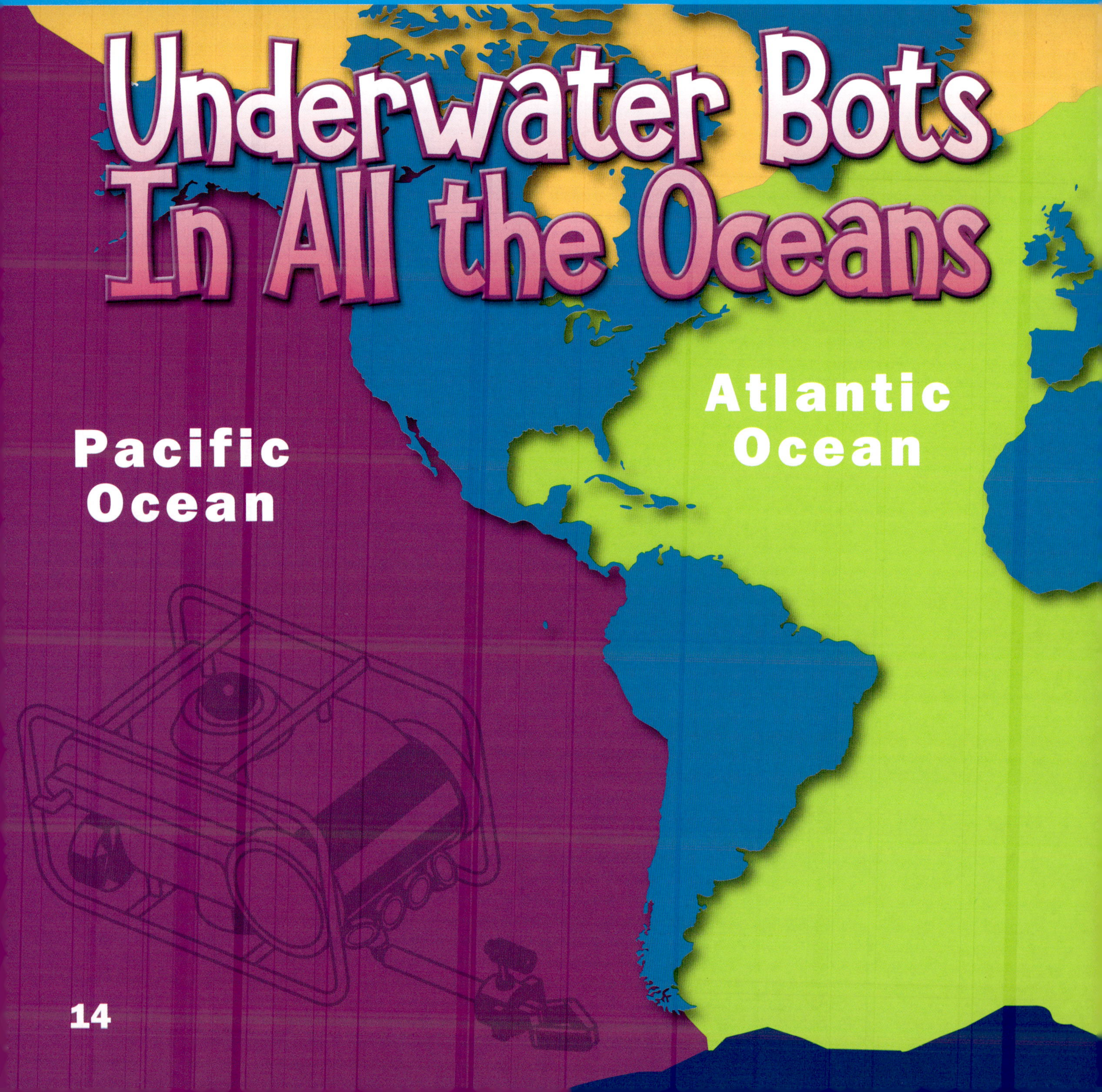

Arctic Ocean
Pacific Ocean
Indian Ocean
Antarctic Ocean

CHAPTER 3

Exploring Oceans

Bots can explore where people can't. Sometimes they carry cameras. People send them into shipwrecks. The bots send pictures back.

FACT
Bots explored the Titanic.

New Life

Scientists use bots to learn about animals too. They let people study sharks. They help discover new animals too.

Oceans are huge. What might bots find next?

Casper Octopus
discovered with a bot

Bonus Facts

One bot traveled 9,000 miles (14,484 kilometers).

Some bots have arms. They fix pipes underwater.

Seaglider can go 19,685 feet (6,000 m) deep.

Some bots are remote-controlled.

remote-controlled: told what to do by something from a distance

READ MORE/WEBSITES

Gagne, Tammy. *Robots.* 21st Century Inventions. Minneapolis: Cody Koala, an imprint of POP, 2019.

Manalang, Dana. *ROPOS and the Underwater Volcano.* Herndon, VA: Mascot Books, 2018.

Troupe, Thomas Kingsley. *Underwater Robots.* Mighty Bots. Mankato, MN: Black Rabbit Books, 2018.

Robotics
kidsahead.com/subjects/1-robotics

Robotics: Facts
idahoptv.org/sciencetrek/topics/robots/facts.cfm

Robots for Kids
www.sciencekids.co.nz/robots.html

GLOSSARY

explore (ek-SPLOR)—to look at and study something

global warming (GLO-buhl WARM-ing)—a warming of Earth's air and oceans

measure (MEH-zhur)—to find out the size or amount of something

remote-controlled (ree-MOT kun-TROLD)—told what to do by something from a distance

trash (TRASH)—things that are no longer wanted

INDEX

C

cleaning, 7, 13

D

discoveries, 7, 19

M

mapping, 13

R

researching, 4, 7, 10, 13, 16, 19

S

Seaglider bots, 8–9, 10, 11, 21